This Ladybird Book belongs to:

Andrew ALLison

From: Nanny:

On your 5th

Birthday.

D0998295

All children have a great ambition ... to read by themselves.

Through traditional and popular stories, each title in the **Read It Yourself** series introduces children to the most commonly used words in the English language (*Key Words*), plus additional words necessary to tell the story.
The additional words appearing in this book are listed below.

Jack, money, food, throws, beanstalk, giant, wife, fee, fi, fo, fum, cupboard, sleep, stole, hen, harp, axe, killed, magic, beans, garden

Ladybird books are widely available, but in case of difficulty may be ordered by post or telephone from: Ladybird Books, Cash Sales Department, Littlegate Road, Paignton, Devon. TQ3 3BE. Telephone 0803 554761.
A catalogue record for this book is available from the British Library.

Revised edition
Published by Ladybird Books Ltd Loughborough Leicestershire UK
Ladybird Books Inc Auburn Maine 04210 USA
Printed in England
© LADYBIRD BOOKS LTD MCMXCIII

Jack and the Beanstalk

by Fran Hunia
illustrated by Brian Price Thomas

Jack and his mummy have
no money and no food
in the house.

All they have is one cow.

She is a good cow,
and she gives lots of milk,
but Jack and his mummy
want food.

"Off you go with the cow. Get some money for it and then we can have some things for tea," says Jack's mummy.

Away Jack goes with the cow. He sees a man.

"What a good cow you have," says the man.

"Yes," says Jack. "She is a good cow, and she gives lots of milk, but we can't keep her. We have to get some money for food."

"I have no money,"
says the man,
"but I have some magic beans.
Please give me the cow,
and you can have
my magic beans."

"That will be good," says Jack.
"Here you are. You have
the cow, and I'll have
the magic beans."

Jack thanks the man
and then he goes home.

Jack gives the magic beans
to his mummy.
"Look," he says.
"We can have beans for tea."

His mummy looks
at the beans.
"Is that all you have?"
she says.
"I don't want beans."

She throws the beans away,
into the garden,
and Jack has to go to bed
with no tea.

The magic beans come up. They make a big, big beanstalk.

"What a big beanstalk," says Jack. "It makes the house and the trees look little. I'll go and see what is up there."

"No," says Jack's mummy. "Keep away, Jack. There will be danger up there."

"Yes," says Jack. "There will be danger, but I have to go and see what is up there."

His mummy lets him go.

Jack goes up and up and up.

He sees the giant's house,
and he wants to go in.

"No, stop,"
says the giant's wife.
"You can't come in here."

"Please let me come in,"
says Jack. "I will be good."

The giant's wife likes children.
So she lets him in.

She gives him
some food and
Jack thanks her.

The giant comes home.
He says, "Fee, fi, fo, fum,
little children, here I come."

The giant's wife puts Jack
in the cupboard.
She says to the giant,
"There are no children here,
but I have some food
for you."

The giant has his tea
and then he says, "Get me
my money bag."

The giant's wife gets him
the money bag,
and then she goes off
to bed.

Jack looks at the money bag. "The giant stole that money bag from my daddy," he says. "I have to get it."

The giant goes to sleep
and Jack gets
the money bag.

He runs away
down the beanstalk with it.
The giant sleeps on.

Jack gives the money bag
to his mummy.
"Was this daddy's money
bag?" he says.

"Yes, it was,"
says his mummy.
"The giant stole it."

Jack goes up
the beanstalk again.

He comes to
the giant's house,
and sees
the giant's wife.

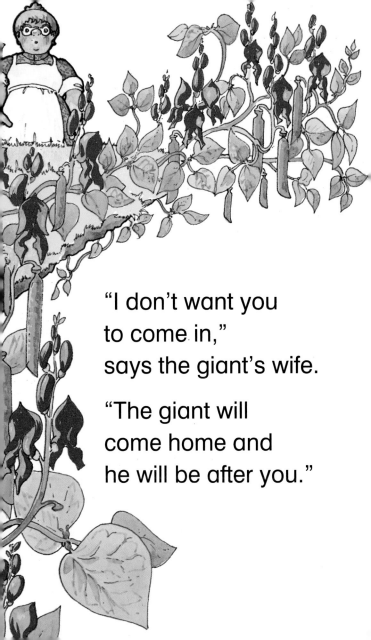

"I don't want you
to come in,"
says the giant's wife.

"The giant will
come home and
he will be after you."

"Please let me in," says Jack.

The giant's wife likes Jack.
She lets him in
and gives him some food
and milk.

Then the giant comes home.
He says, "Fee, fi, fo, fum,
little children, here I come."

Jack gets into the cupboard.

"There are no children here,"
says the giant's wife,
"but I have some food
for you."

The giant has his tea,
and then he says,
"Get me my magic hen."

The giant's wife gives it to him
and then she goes off
to bed.

Jack sees the magic hen.

"The giant stole that hen from my daddy," he says. "I have to get it."

The giant goes to sleep, then Jack gets the hen and runs away with it.

The giant sleeps on.

Jack goes down
the beanstalk.
He gives the hen
to his mummy.

"Can we keep this hen?"
he asks.

"Yes," says his mummy.
"The giant stole that hen
from daddy."

Jack goes up the beanstalk
again and goes
to the giant's house.

"Please go away,"
says the giant's wife.
"You can't come in here.
The giant will get you."

But she wants to help Jack,
so she lets him come in.

The giant comes home.

He says, "Fee, fi, fo, fum,
little children, here I come."

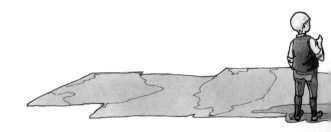

"There are no children here," says the giant's wife, "but I have some food for you."

She gives the giant his tea.

The giant says, "Get me my magic harp."

The giant's wife gives it to him and then she goes off to bed.

The magic harp plays
for the giant,
and he goes to sleep.

Jack looks at the harp.
"That was my daddy's harp,"
he says. "I will get it."

Jack gets the magic harp
and runs off,
but the harp says, "Help, help!"

The giant runs after Jack.

Jack runs to the beanstalk
and the giant runs after him.

Down goes Jack
and down goes the giant.

Jack sees his home.

He says, "Mummy, mummy, get
the axe. The giant is after me."

Jack's mummy runs to get
the axe. She gives it to him.

Down comes the beanstalk
and the giant is killed.

"That is good," says Jack's
mummy. "The giant is
no danger to us now.
Let us go and get
some good things for tea."

LADYBIRD
READING SCHEMES

Read It Yourself links with all Ladybird reading schemes and can be used with any other method of learning to read.

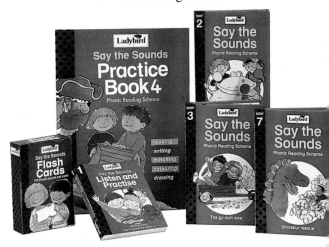

Say the Sounds

Ladybird's **Say the Sounds** graded reading scheme is a *phonics* scheme. It teaches children the sounds of individual letters and letter combinations, enabling them to tackle new words by building them up as a blend of smaller units.

There are 8 titles in this scheme:

1 **Rocket to the jungle**
2 **Frog and the lollipops**
3 **The go-cart race**
4 **Pirate's treasure**
5 **Humpty Dumpty and the robot**
6 **Flying saucer**
7 **Dinosaur rescue**
8 **The accident**

Support material available: Practice Books, Double Cassette pack, Flash Cards